ALAN SNOW'S Wacky GUIDE TO PaperFun

WALKER BOOKS
LONDON

Dear Paperologist

Paper, as you are soon to learn, is extraordinarily useful stuff. In fact, if I was stranded on a desert island and could only take one thing, paper is what I would ask for. You can wear it, make noises with it, play games with it, drink out of it. There's even a kind you can eat!

To become a skilled paperologist like me you'll need to remember these 4 important rules.

1. If you are going to make a mess, make sure you cover your work surface with newspaper, wear your oldest clothes and tidy up afterwards.

2. Read the list of things you need before you start and make sure you have everything.

3. When you see this sign, ask a grown-up to help you.

4. Only use round-ended scissors and be very, very careful.

See you on a desert island (don't forget the paper!).

Alan Snow

Contents

Fakes and Forgeries 4-5

Incredible Indoor Sports (1st Half) 6-7

Top Secret 8-9

Your Very Own Personal
Printing Press 10-11

How to Build Your Own Airline 12-13

Moving Pictures (Act One) 14-15

Newspapers 16-17

Build Your Own Fleet of Ships 18-19

Instant Art 20-21

DIY Hullabaloo 22-23

Dressing Up 24-25

Moving Pictures (Act Two) 26-27

Incredible Indoor Sports (2nd Half) 28-29

The Really Useful and Really
Naughty Origami Page 30-31

Pictures You Can Eat 32

Ye Olde Paper

You will need some sheets of white paper, a ruler, a pot of cold tea, a washing-up bowl, a thin paintbrush and a little vegetable oil.

Making The Edges of The Paper Look Old ①

Place the ruler 1 cm from the edge of the paper and tear off a strip. Tear strips off the other edges in the same way.

How to make ye olde treasure maps.

Browning and Ageing ②

Put the sheets of torn paper in the washing-up bowl and pour on the tea.

Make sure the paper is covered. Wait for 15 minutes.

Then remove the paper and hang it up to dry.

Making a Watermark ③

If you hold paper money or writing paper up to the light, you may see a design in the paper. This is a watermark, put there by the paper maker. To make your own watermark, dip the paintbrush into the oil and draw a design very lightly on the paper.

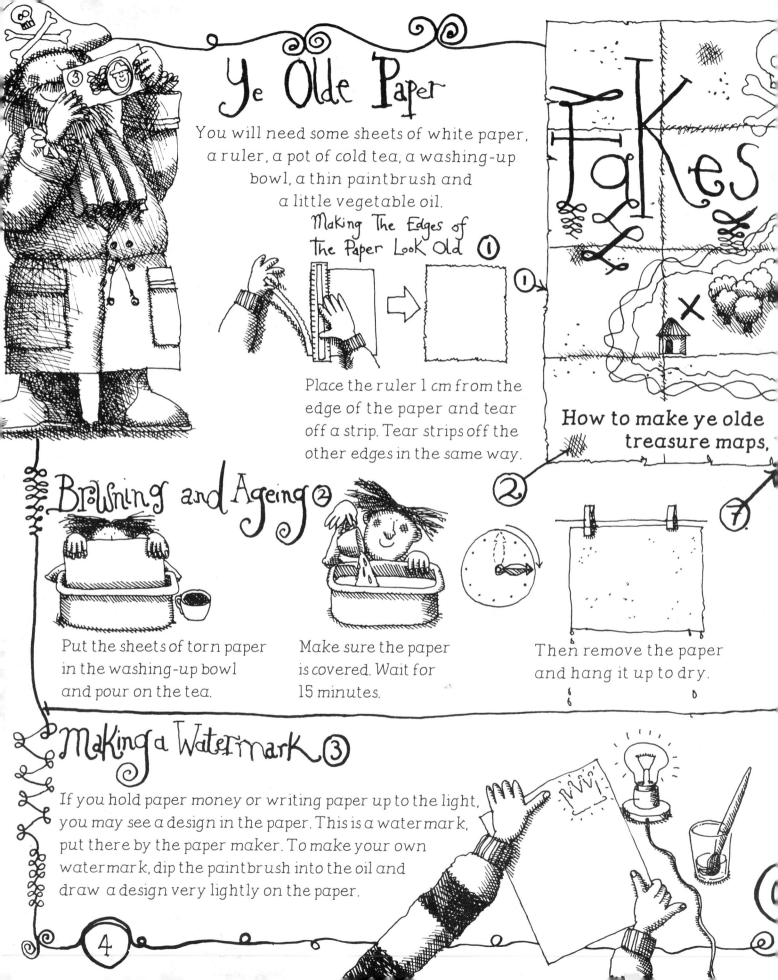

Ye Olde Writing

You will need a drinking straw or a feather, scissors, black ink, some kitchen paper, a thin paintbrush and some red paint.

Making a quill pen

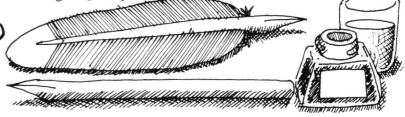

Before pens were invented, people cut the tips off feathers to make nibs and then dipped the nibs into ink. When the nibs got blunt they just cut a bit more off the feathers. Make your own quill pen by cutting a drinking straw at a sharp angle to make a nib. Better still, use a feather!

③

⑤

...and Forgeries

documents – letters, even paper money!

ye Signature ⑥

④

Writing

Dip the nib into the ink and write or draw on ye olde paper.

Soak up extra ink by putting a sheet of kitchen paper lightly on top of the paper. This is called "blotting".

Add lots of fancy decoration – curls, whirls, patterns, squiggles, even ink splodges! ④

In olden days people used to write a small "f" instead of a small "s". Try it! ⑤

Very important documents were sometimes signed in blood! Use a thin paint-brush and some red paint for "blood" signatures. ⑥

Creasing and Folding ⑦

To make your document look really old, spend 5 minutes folding and unfolding it. Then flatten it out.

Hiding Ye Fakes and Forgeries

Fold up your document, or roll it up and tie it with a ribbon. Then hide it where you are sure it will be found by the person you want to find it!

Bat-a-Rat a game for 2 or more

You need 2 newspapers, sticky tape, a chair and some small, unbreakable objects ("rats").

1. Roll up one of the newspapers quite loosely and tape it to make a tube.

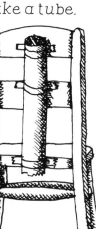

2. Tape the tube to the back of the chair.

3. Fold the other newspaper in half, roll it up and tape it to make the bat.

4. One player drops the rats, one at a time, down the tube. The other player tries to hit them with the bat as they fall out of the bottom. After 10 goes, the batter swaps places with the dropper. Keep a score of hits.

Incred Indoor

Cornflakes Football

a game for 2 or more

You need an empty cornflakes packet, sticky tape, glue, sheets of paper and scissors. Use a table or the floor for your pitch.

1. Cut the cereal packet in half to make the 2 goals.

2. Cut the front out of each goal.

3. Put the goals at each end of your pitch and tape.

4. To make a blower for each player, roll up a sheet of paper into a tube and tape.

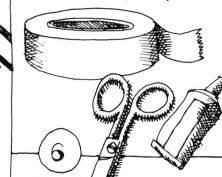

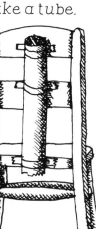

6

ible Sports
(1st Half)

Matchbox Relay
a race for 2 teams

You need the sleeves of 2 matchboxes.

1. The 2 teams stand in line. The first person in each team puts a matchbox sleeve on his or her nose.

2. On the word "go" the players pass the sleeve along the line using noses only. If a player drops the sleeve, the team has to start again. The first team to pass the sleeve to the end of the line is the winner!

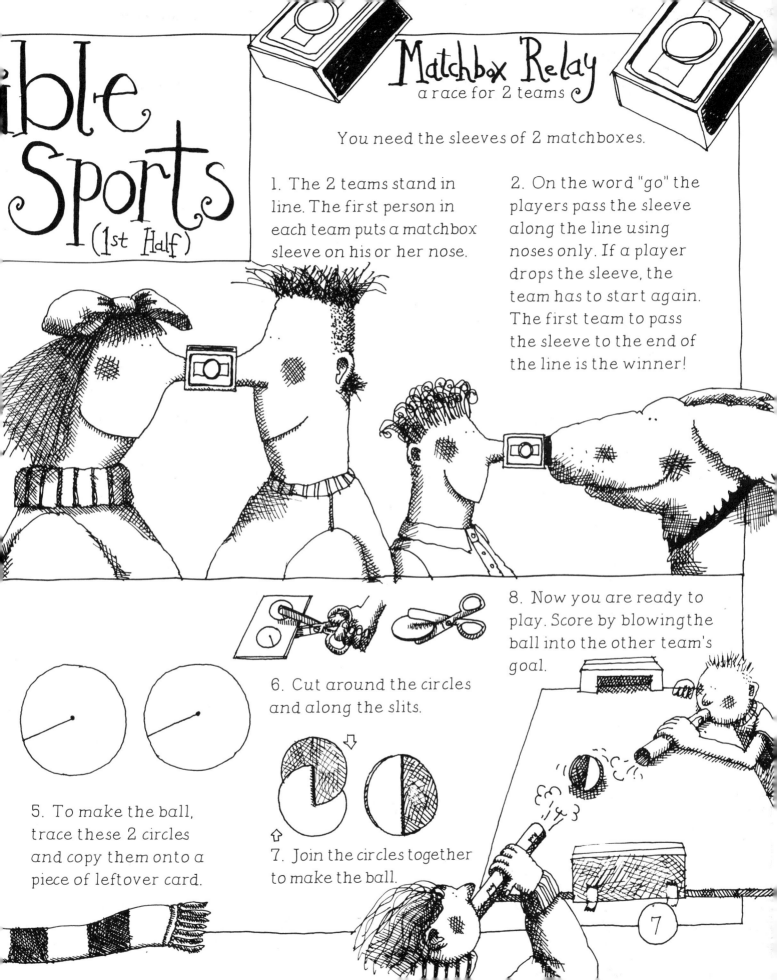

8. Now you are ready to play. Score by blowing the ball into the other team's goal.

6. Cut around the circles and along the slits.

5. To make the ball, trace these 2 circles and copy them onto a piece of leftover card.

7. Join the circles together to make the ball.

Special Spy Name

Invent a secret spy name for yourself. Only tell friendly spies what it is.

Invisible Writing

How to pass secret messages to friendly spies on blank sheets of paper!

You will need half a lemon, a lemon squeezer, a saucer, a thin paintbrush and a sheet of white paper.

1. Squeeze the lemon-half and pour the juice into a saucer.

2. Dip your brush into the juice and write a message on the sheet of paper. Sign it with your secret name.

3. Leave the sheet of paper to dry. The message will disappear!

4. Tell your friendly spy to put the sheet of paper in a low oven and wait for about 10 minutes. Then take it out of the oven. The lemon-juice writing will now be brown so your message can be read!

Top

Some crucial tricks of

Phoney Voices!

Two ways to make your voice sound different on the phone. ALWAYS ask first before you make a call.

The Long Distance Caller

Scrumple up a piece of paper, hold it *close* to the mouthpiece of the phone and dial the number you want. When the phone is answered, carry on scrumpling while you speak.

The Muffled Voice

Fold a sheet of writing paper into several layers and hold it over your mouth when you make a phone call. Your voice will sound very odd indeed!

Secret

the trade for spies.

Here are 3 ways of writing messages to a friendly spy in code. Try sending messages in code <u>and</u> in invisible writing.

The Really Easy Alpha Code!

Use a number instead of a letter.
It's important to leave a space between numbers and a bigger space between words.

A	B	C	D	E	F	G	H	I	J	K	L	M	N	O	P	Q	R	S	T	U	V	W	X	Y	Z
1	2	3	4	5	6	7	8	9	10	11	12	13	14	15	16	17	18	19	20	21	22	23	24	25	26

8 5 12 12 15, 6 18 9 5 14 12 25 19 16 25.   (HELLO, FRIENDLY SPY.)

Top-Secret Book Code

This is one of the hardest codes in the world to crack!
You'll each need an identical copy of the same book.

Write a message and then look through the book to find the words. Make a note of the page, line and word numbers and then send a message like this:

48 4 3 / 23 1 4 / 11 5 6
(sausages   for   tea)

Remember that a printed picture is the mirror image of the design you make on the printing block, so letters and numbers should be written backwards. Check your designs in a mirror.

Potato Prints

You need a medium-sized baking potato, a round-bladed knife, a teaspoon, some sheets of paper, poster paint, kitchen paper and a plate.

1. Cut the potato in half to make 2 printing blocks.

2. Carve a design into one potato-half, using the knife and the teaspoon.

3. You can also carve a potato-half into a shape.

4. Spread a thin layer of paint over the flat surface of the plate.

5. Rub the potato-half into the paint.

6. To print, carefully press the potato-half down onto a sheet of paper.

7. Lift off the potato-half.

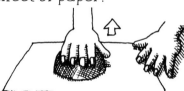

8. Print your design as many times as you like. Try using different colours and types of paper, but wash the potato-halves between colours and dry them on kitchen paper.

It's good for crowd scenes!

String Prints

You need some cardboard, scissors, a felt-tip pen, Copydex, some thick poster paint, some thin string, a plate and some sheets of paper.

Mono Prints

"Mono" means single or one. You can only print your design once using this method.

You need a plate, a paintbrush, some thick poster paint, scissors and paper.

1. Draw a circle on the paper the same size as the flat part of the plate and cut it out.

10

Own Personal Press

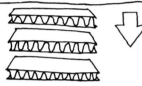

1. Cut out 3 identical pieces of cardboard, each one slightly smaller than the flat part of the plate. Glue them together to make a printing block.

2. Draw a simple design on one side of the block.

3. Paint over the design with Copydex.

4. Wait until you can see through the glue. Then stick pieces of string along the lines, pressing them into the glue. Let it dry.

5. Meanwhile spread a thin layer of paint on the plate.

6. Gently press the block into the paint.

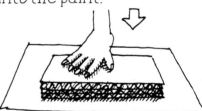

7. Check that the string is now covered in paint and then press the block onto the paper.

8. Lift the block off the paper. Hey presto!

2. Spread a thin layer of paint onto the flat part of the plate and scratch a design into it with the wrong end of the paintbrush. Cut out paper shapes and press them into the paint for bigger areas that you want to keep blank.

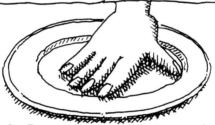

3. Put the round piece of paper onto the plate and gently press it into the paint.

4. Carefully pull the paper off the plate and let it dry.

5. Wash and dry the plate and start again.

The Super-Smooth Jumbo Glider

You need a piece of writing paper.

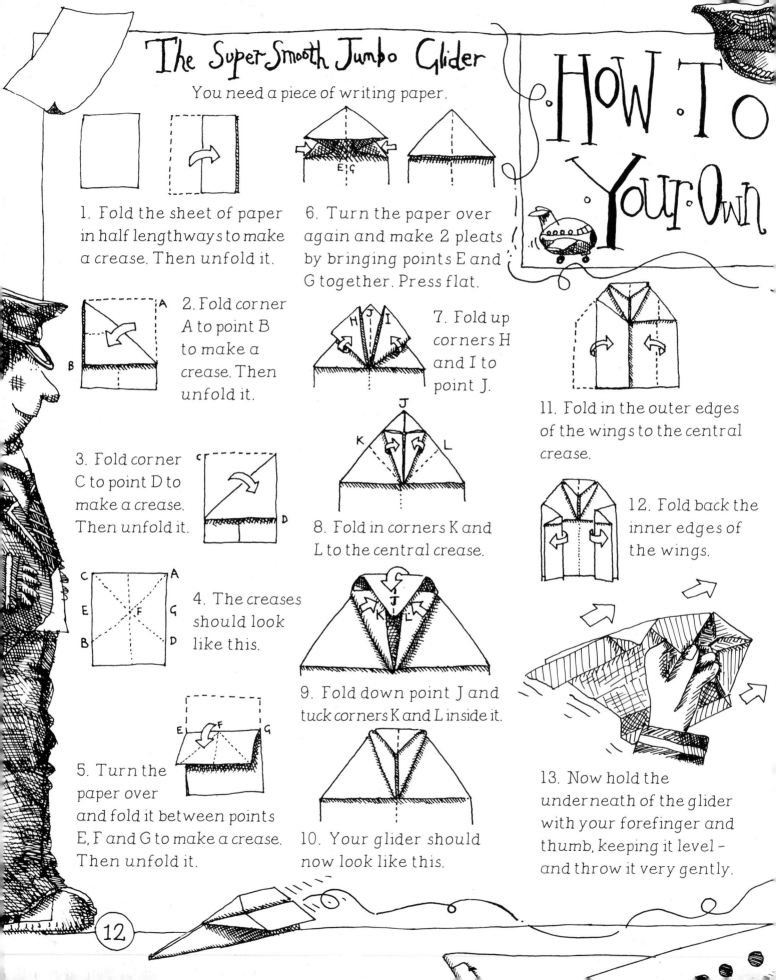

1. Fold the sheet of paper in half lengthways to make a crease. Then unfold it.

2. Fold corner A to point B to make a crease. Then unfold it.

3. Fold corner C to point D to make a crease. Then unfold it.

4. The creases should look like this.

5. Turn the paper over and fold it between points E, F and G to make a crease. Then unfold it.

6. Turn the paper over again and make 2 pleats by bringing points E and G together. Press flat.

7. Fold up corners H and I to point J.

8. Fold in corners K and L to the central crease.

9. Fold down point J and tuck corners K and L inside it.

10. Your glider should now look like this.

11. Fold in the outer edges of the wings to the central crease.

12. Fold back the inner edges of the wings.

13. Now hold the underneath of the glider with your forefinger and thumb, keeping it level – and throw it very gently.

Build Airline

Aircraft Hangar

A game to play with friends or on your own.

You need 4 wire coat-hangers, some sticky tape, a piece of string, an open door and an airline!

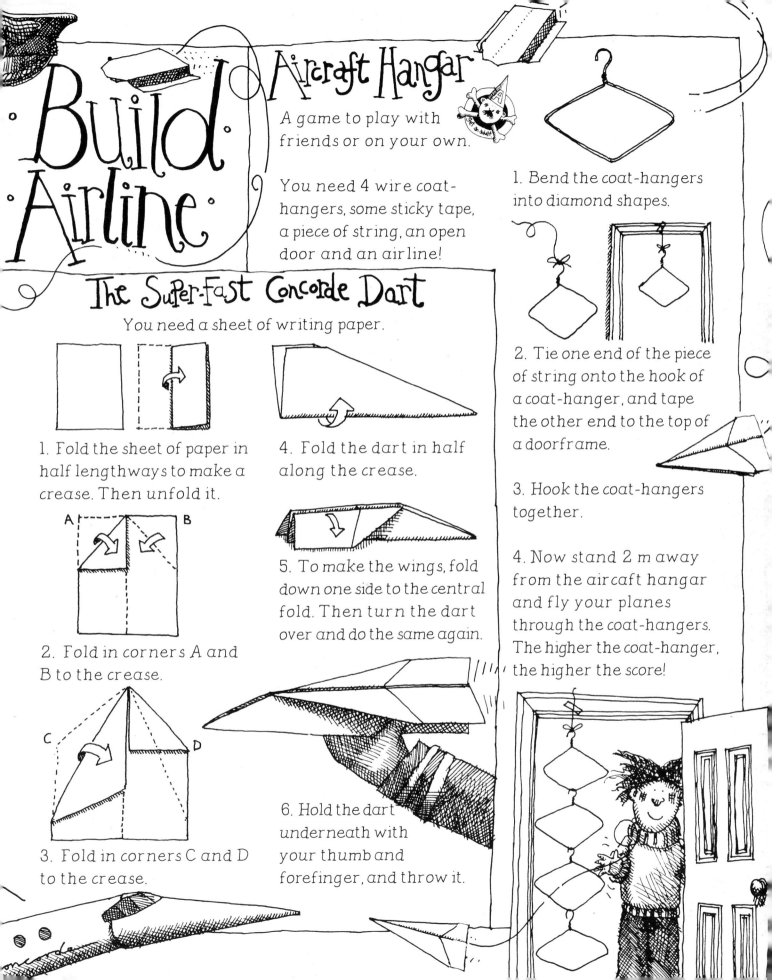

1. Bend the coat-hangers into diamond shapes.

2. Tie one end of the piece of string onto the hook of a coat-hanger, and tape the other end to the top of a doorframe.

3. Hook the coat-hangers together.

4. Now stand 2 m away from the aircaft hangar and fly your planes through the coat-hangers. The higher the coat-hanger, the higher the score!

The Super-Fast Concorde Dart

You need a sheet of writing paper.

1. Fold the sheet of paper in half lengthways to make a crease. Then unfold it.

2. Fold in corners A and B to the crease.

3. Fold in corners C and D to the crease.

4. Fold the dart in half along the crease.

5. To make the wings, fold down one side to the central fold. Then turn the dart over and do the same again.

6. Hold the dart underneath with your thumb and forefinger, and throw it.

The Smallest Theatre in the World

Moving

You need an empty matchbox, scissors and a felt-tip pen.

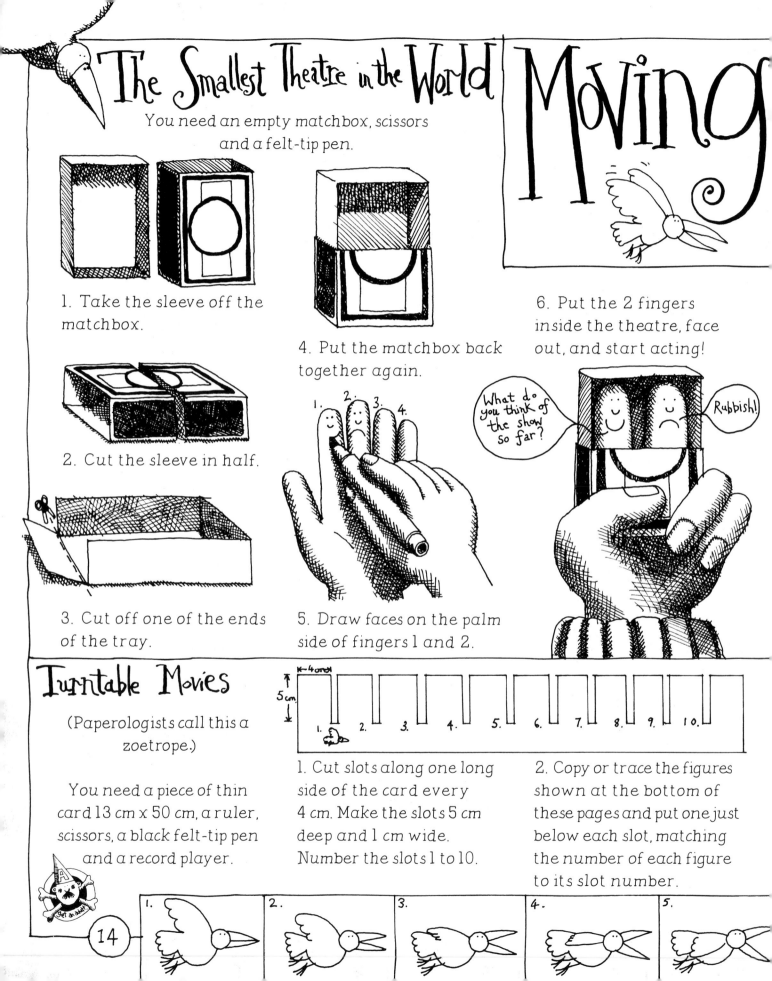

1. Take the sleeve off the matchbox.

2. Cut the sleeve in half.

3. Cut off one of the ends of the tray.

4. Put the matchbox back together again.

5. Draw faces on the palm side of fingers 1 and 2.

6. Put the 2 fingers inside the theatre, face out, and start acting!

What do you think of the show so far?

Rubbish!

Turntable Movies

(Paperologists call this a zoetrope.)

You need a piece of thin card 13 cm x 50 cm, a ruler, scissors, a black felt-tip pen and a record player.

1. Cut slots along one long side of the card every 4 cm. Make the slots 5 cm deep and 1 cm wide. Number the slots 1 to 10.

2. Copy or trace the figures shown at the bottom of these pages and put one just below each slot, matching the number of each figure to its slot number.

14

Pictures (Act One)

Rainbow Spinner

You need a piece of card slightly bigger than a saucer, a piece of string 1.5 m long, a ruler, a selection of coloured felt-tip pens or crayons, scissors and a saucer.

1. Put the saucer upside down on the card and draw around it.
2. Cut out the circle.

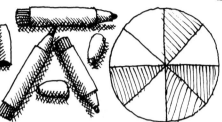

3. With the ruler and a crayon or felt-tip pen, divide the circle into 8 segments on both sides and colour in each segment.

4. Punch 2 holes, one on either side of the centre of the circle. Thread one end of the string through a hole and make a big loop. Thread the other end of the string back again through the second hole on the other side. Tie the 2 ends with a knot.

5. Put your forefingers through the loops of string on either side of the circle and swing the circle over and over to wind it up.

6. Now pull your hands apart and watch the show!

3. Bend the card into a circle with the pictures on the inside, and tape.

4. Place the circle on the turntable of the record player.

5. Stand or sit with your eyes level with the bottom of the slots, switch on the turntable and watch the movie!

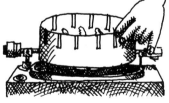

7.	8.	9.	10.

Giant Prize Marrow!

You need a long, outsize balloon, some newspaper, a washing-up bowl, water, a pin, wallpaper paste, poster paints, a paintbrush and varnish.

Don't just read them –

1. Tear the newspaper into strips and put them in a washing-up bowl filled with water. Add a tablespoon of dry wallpaper paste to the water. Leave it to soak for a couple of hours.

2. Blow up the balloon.

3. Cover the ballooon in several layers of soaked newspaper, leaving the tied end of the balloon sticking out. Leave it to dry.

4. When it is almost dry, add some more layers. Let it dry out completely.

5. Burst the balloon with the pin and pull it out by the tied end.

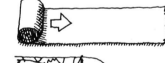

6. Roll up some strips of soaked newspaper to make a stalk and glue it onto the end.

7. Paint the marrow, making it look as real as possible. When it is dry, paint on a layer of varnish.

Show off the marrow to your friends. They will think you are an ace gardener! Think of other giant fruit and vegetables to make out of balloons of different shapes and sizes.

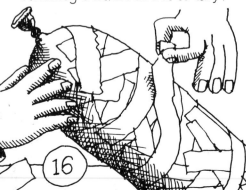

aPers

DO things with them!

Tree Trick

Everyone knows that paper is made out of trees, but did you know you can make trees out of paper?

You need a sheet of newspaper, scissors and sticky tape.

1. Open out a sheet of newspaper and cut it in half widthways.

2. Roll it up fairly loosely and tape.

3. Make 5 or 6 cuts in the roll about 15 cm long.

4. Bend the cut flaps down.

5. Hold the stump with one hand. With the other hand gently pull out the inside sections as far as you can to make your tree grow!

Extraordinary Expanding Ladder

You need 3 sheets of newspaper, scissors and sticky tape.

1. Open up the sheets of newspaper and tape them together.

2. Roll them up and tape as shown.

3. Flatten the roll and cut out the section shown in the picture, leaving a bridge about 3 cm wide between the ends.

4. Bend the ends downwards.

5. Gently pull up the insides of the 2 ends, one at a time, until the ladder has expanded as far as it will go.

H.M.S. Fleet Street

You need a page from a newspaper and some sticky tape.

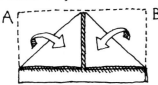

1. Fold the paper in half widthways.

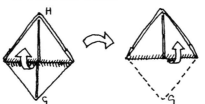

2. Fold in corners A and B to meet in the centre.

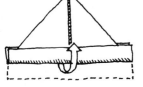

3. Fold up the bottom flap. Turn the ship over and fold up the other flap.

4. Fold corners C and D down and tape. Turn the ship over and do the same to the other side.

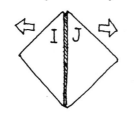

5. Take hold of points E and F and push them together.

6. The ship should now look like this.

7. Fold point G up to point H. Turn the ship over and do this again on the other side.

8. Repeat step 5.

9. Hold points I and J and pull gently.

Hey presto! A ship for your fleet.

The Boat Race

You need some silver paper, scissors, a ball-point pen and some washing-up liquid.

1. Cut out small, boat-shaped pieces of silver paper, one for each sailor. Label each boat with its sailor's name.

2. Make sure the water is quite still by putting a small piece of paper on it. If it doesn't move, the water is still.

Own Fleet

and launch them in your bath!

3. Carefully line up the silver-paper boats on the water at one end of the bath.

4. Put a couple of drops of washing-up liquid into the water behind the boats and watch them zoom towards the other end. The winner is the one that goes the furthest.

5. Remember to change the water between races.

Bath Tub Barges

You need some clean empty milk or juice cartons, scissors, string and some freight to put in your barges – small toys for example.

1. Cut the cartons in half, keeping the bottom halves for your barges.

2. Make 2 holes in the ends of each barge, near the top.

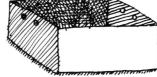

3. Join 2 barges together with a piece of string about 20 cm long. Thread the string through the holes in both barges and tie the ends together. Add on as many barges as you like in the same way.

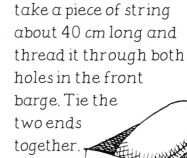

4. To make a tow-rope, take a piece of string about 40 cm long and thread it through both holes in the front barge. Tie the two ends together.

5. Now load up your barges and tow them around the bath!

19

Oily Patterns

You need 2 different-coloured poster paints, 2 small yogurt pots, a teaspoon, some cooking oil, a shallow dish containing about 1 cm water and some sheets of paper which are slightly smaller than the dish.

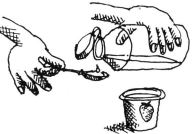

1. Using a different colour in each yogurt pot, mix up some fairly thick paint and add a teaspoon of cooking oil.

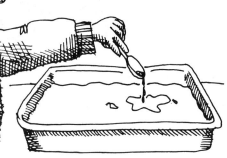

2. With the teaspoon, dribble the paint mixture into the water, one colour at a time.

3. Stir gently for a moment.

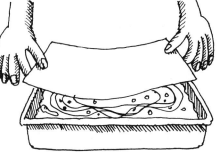

4. Float a sheet of paper on the surface of the water and wait for the paper to absorb some of the paint mixture.

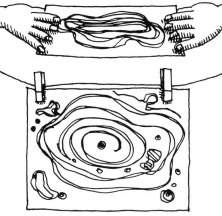

5. Remove the paper, keeping it level so the paint cannot run. Let the paper dry.

6. Experiment with different amounts of paint, oil and stirring. Each time you will get a different result.

Instant A.f. D.I.Y. Scraperboard

You need some wax crayons, black poster paint, a paint-brush, some sheets of paper, a straightened paper-clip and washing-up liquid.

1. Scribble all over a sheet of paper with the wax crayons so that it is covered in a layer of coloured wax.

2. Mix up some quite thick black paint and add a squirt of washing-up liquid.

20

Art

3. Paint all over the coloured wax with the black paint mixture and let it dry.

4. With the straightened paper-clip, scratch a design into the black paint. The coloured wax will show through.

Making Copies

How to copy a picture and how to change the size of your copy.

You need a picture to copy, a ruler, a pencil, a rubber, scissors and a large sheet of paper.

Bigger and Smaller

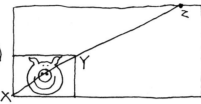

1. Put the picture you want to copy in the bottom, left-hand corner of the sheet of paper. Put the ruler diagonally across it and the paper and draw a line between Y and Z.

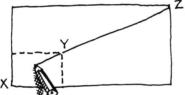

2. Remove the picture and complete the line between X and Y.

3. Decide how big you want your copy to be and then draw a line between A and B and then B and C.

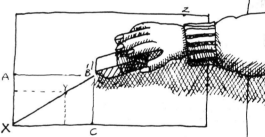

4. This is the area for your copy. Rub out the diagonal line and cut it out.

Copying

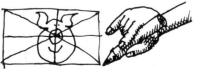

1. Using a pencil and ruler, draw a grid over the picture like this.

2. Draw an identical grid over the sheet of paper.

3. Now copy the picture, section by section.

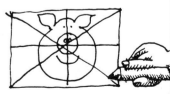

4. Finally, carefully rub out the grid lines. You can now colour in your copy.

The Rootin' Tootin' Hooter

You need a plastic drinking straw, scissors, sticky tape and a postcard.

1. Flatten the straw about 3 cm from one end.

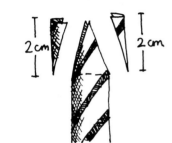

2. Cut a beak-shaped mouthpiece.

3. Put the straw on its side and flatten it again. Then cut 3 small, triangular notches in one flattened edge.

4. Roll the postcard into a cone-shape and tape.

5. Flatten the cone and cut off the tip, making a hole big enough to fit the straw through. Trim the bottom edge as well.

6. Unflatten the cone and put the end of the straw through the hole in the tip. Attach the cone to the straw with sticky tape wrapped round and round.

Nice, noisy

7. Put the mouthpiece between your lips, and your fingers over the holes.

8. Blow hard and lift up your fingers, 1, 2 or 3 at a time, rather like playing a recorder.

toot toot toot

Yaloo!

noises!

Frog Croaker

You need a paper cup and a comb.

Hold the comb on the bottom of the cup, teeth upwards, and flick the teeth with your thumb.

Ribbet-Ribbet

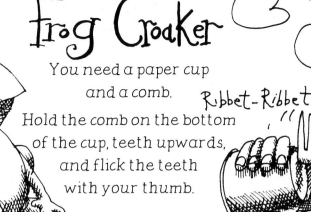

Krazy Kazoo!

You need a short cardboard tube, scissors, a sharp pencil, an elastic band and a piece of greaseproof paper.

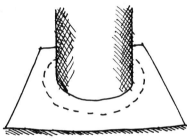

1. Cut out a piece of greaseproof paper a bit bigger than the end of the tube.

2. Cover one end of the tube with the greaseproof paper and hold it in position with the elastic band.

3. With the pencil, punch a small hole in the tube about 3 cm from the top.

4. Put your mouth close to the hole and toot a tune into it, high and loud.

Zoot — Zoot — Zoot

Hummy Comb

You need a comb and a small sheet of greaseproof paper.

1. Fold the piece of paper over the comb.

2. Hold the comb close to your mouth and hum a tune with your mouth open and blowing slightly.

BUZZ

HUM

The Wonderful World of Wigs

You need some thin card, a ruler, sticky tape, glue, scissors and paper.

1. Cut a strip of card, long enough to fit around your head and 2.5 cm wide. Bend it into a circle and tape.

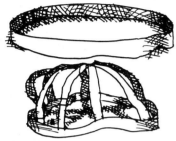

2. Cut out 4 strips of card, long enough to go over your head and 1.5 cm wide. Tape them to the circle of card to make the wig base.

3. To make the hair, cut out strips of paper 20 cm long and 1cm wide. Rub the strips of paper with the blades of a pair of closed scissors to make them curl.

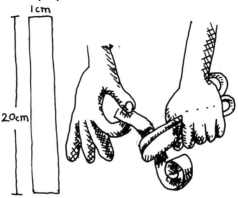

Dressing

Smarten up with these to make a wig, jewellery, a them with paints, coloured like. To make a real impact,

4. Now glue the curls on to the wig base.

5. Trim to taste!

The Bouncing-Bow Tie

You need some card, scissors, a pencil, a ruler, sticky tape and elastic.

1. Cut out a bow-tie shape to the size you want.

2. Cut out a piece of card 3 cm x 1.5 cm. Punch a hole at either end and tape it onto the back of the bow-tie.

3. Cut out another strip of card and wrap it around the middle of the bow-tie. Tape at the back.

4. Cut a piece of elastic, long enough to go round your neck. Thread it through the holes and tie knots at both ends.

5. Now decorate the bow-tie and put it on.

UP

wicked fashion tips – how [to make a] mask and a tie. Decorate [your] paper, food – anything you [can] wear them all at once!

Sunday Supplement Beads

You need a colour magazine, scissors, glue, and some string.

1. Choose a colourful page and cut it into long thin triangular strips.

2. Starting at the wide end, roll up the strips.

3. Put some glue on the pointed end of the strip and stick. Make as many beads as you need.

4. Now make a necklace. Cut a piece of string long enough for a necklace. Tie a knot at one end and thread the beads onto it. Tie the ends of the string together.

5. To make a bracelet, cut a piece of string long enough to go around your wrist. Thread beads onto it and tie the ends together.

The Almost Instant Mask

You need a paper plate, scissors, a sheet of paper, elastic and a pencil.

1. Fold the sheet of paper in half and hold it in front of one half of your face. Look in a mirror. With the pencil, mark the position of holes for your eyes, nose and mouth.

2. Cut out the holes.

3. Flatten the sheet of paper and put it on the paper plate. Draw on the holes and then cut them out.

4. Soak the mask in cold water for 5 minutes and then mould it on to your face. Remove the mask and let it dry.

5. Punch a hole in either side of the mask. Cut a piece of elastic long enough to go round your head, thread it through the holes and tie a knot at each end.

6. Decorate the mask and wear it.

Finger Wiggle Circus

You need two 6 cm x 6 cm pieces of thin card, crayons and scissors.

1. Draw the the front view of an elephant on one piece of card, minus a trunk. Draw a circle where the trunk should go, big enough to make a hole to stick your finger through.

3. Draw the front view of a clown on the other piece of card. Draw 2 circles for holes to stick your fingers through to make legs.

2. Cut out the elephant and make the hole for the trunk.

4. Cut out the clown and make the 2 holes for the legs.

5. Put the forefinger of one hand through the hole in the elephant. Put 2 fingers of the other hand through the holes in the clown. Now wiggle your fingers.

Catch a Burglar Spinner

You need a 7 cm x 7 cm piece of card, 2 pieces of string 30 cm long, scissors and a pencil.

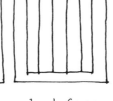

1. Draw a burglar's face on one side of the card and a prison window on the other side.

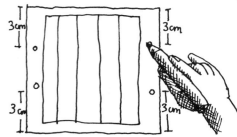

2. With a pencil, make 2 holes on either side of the card 3 cm from the top and the bottom.

26

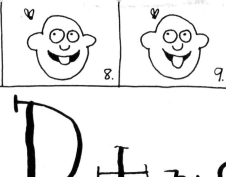
Pictures (Act Two)

Crazy Flicker Book

(Use the pictures at the top and bottom of these pages.)
You need a small note pad, some tracing paper and a pencil.

1. Copy or trace picture 1 onto the bottom right-hand corner of the last page in your note pad.

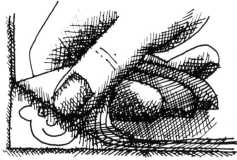

2. Copy or trace picture 2 onto the second from last page, and so on until you have put all the pictures into the note pad. Make sure you always put the picture in the same place on each page.

3. Starting at the back of the note pad, flick forwards through the pages with your thumb. Watch the crazy face catch and eat the bug before your very eyes. Start flicking from the front of the book to make your movie go backwards!

3. Tie the pieces of string on to the card to make 2 loops.

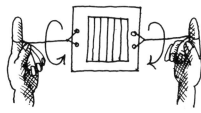

4. Put your forefingers through the each of the loops and swing the card over and over to wind it up.

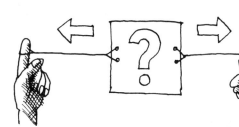

5. Now pull on the string and watch the card unwind. You've put the burglar behind bars!

Whack-a-Fish

a race for 2 or more

You need a newspaper for each player and a largish floor to use as a racetrack.

1. Cut out a fish from a half a sheet of newspaper for each player.

2. Fold the rest of the newspaper in half to make a whacker. Make a whacker for each player.

3. Line up the fish on the floor.

4. On the word "go" whack your whacker behind your fish and the fish will be blown across the floor. The first fish to reach the finishing line is the winner.

A Newspaper Ball

for indoor sports

You need a newspaper, scissors and some sticky tape.

1. Cut sheets of newspaper into strips.

2. Scrumple up 4 or 5 strips into a ball.

3. Wind the other strips around the ball. Tape from time to time to stop it coming undone.

4. When the ball is the size you want, finish it off by winding sticky tape around it.

Indoor
(2nd Half)

Paper Plate Tennis

a game for 2 players
You need 4 paper plates, sticky tape,
a newspaper ball, some string and 2 chairs.

1. To make a racket, put a paper plate face down on top of another one. Tape them together, leaving a gap big enough for 4 fingers. Make a racket for each player.

2. Place the chairs 2 m apart and tie the string between them.

3. Bat the ball to and fro across the string.

Ten Pin Bowling

a game for 2 or more players
You need a newspaper ball, some empty cardboard packets or toilet rolls to make 10 skittles, and a floor to use as a bowling alley.

1. Place the skittles in a triangle pattern at one end of your bowling alley. Put the tallest skittles at the back.

2. Take it in turns to stand at the other end of the bowling alley and roll the ball at the skittles. Each player can have 2 rolls a turn. Keep a score of the number of skittles you knock over with each roll. If you knock over all the skittles in one roll, double your score.

The · Instant · Cup

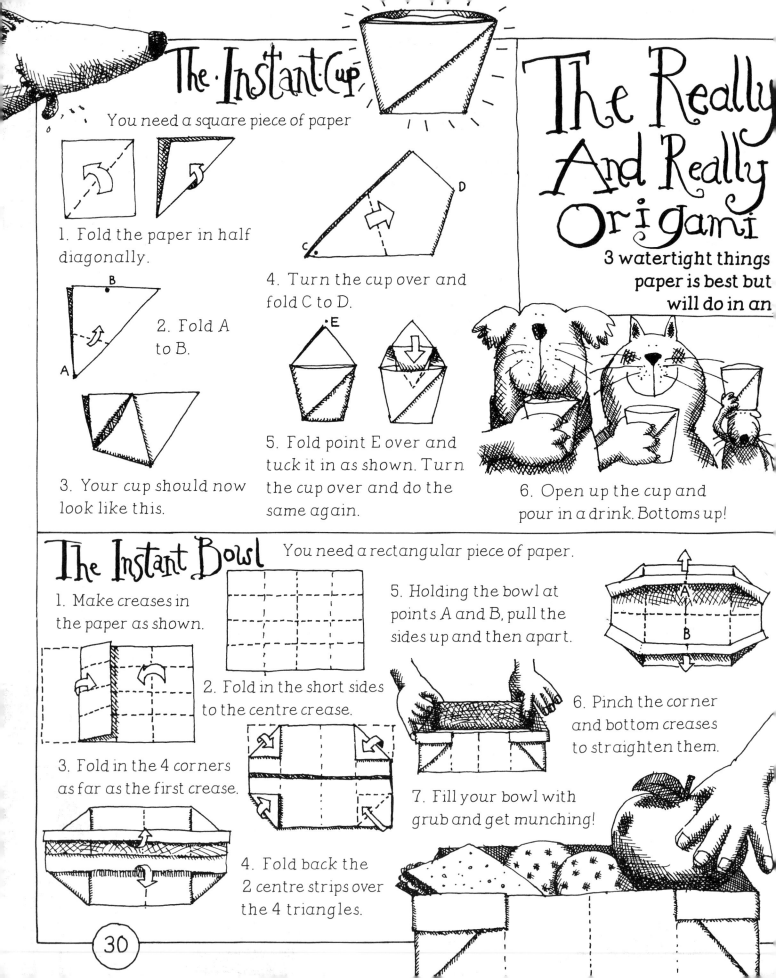

You need a square piece of paper

1. Fold the paper in half diagonally.

2. Fold A to B.

3. Your cup should now look like this.

4. Turn the *cup* over and fold C to D.

5. Fold point E over and tuck it in as shown. Turn the *cup* over and do the same again.

6. Open up the *cup* and pour in a drink. Bottoms up!

The Really And Really Origami

3 watertight things paper is best but will do in an

The Instant Bowl

You need a rectangular piece of paper.

1. Make creases in the paper as shown.

2. Fold in the short sides to the centre crease.

3. Fold in the 4 corners as far as the first crease.

4. Fold back the 2 centre strips over the 4 triangles.

5. Holding the bowl at points A and B, pull the sides up and then apart.

6. Pinch the corner and bottom creases to straighten them.

7. Fill your bowl with grub and get munching!

Useful Naughty Page !!

to make. Greaseproof
ordinary paper
emergency!

The Wicked Water Bomb

You need a square piece of paper
about 20 cm x 20 cm.

1. Make creases in
the paper as shown.

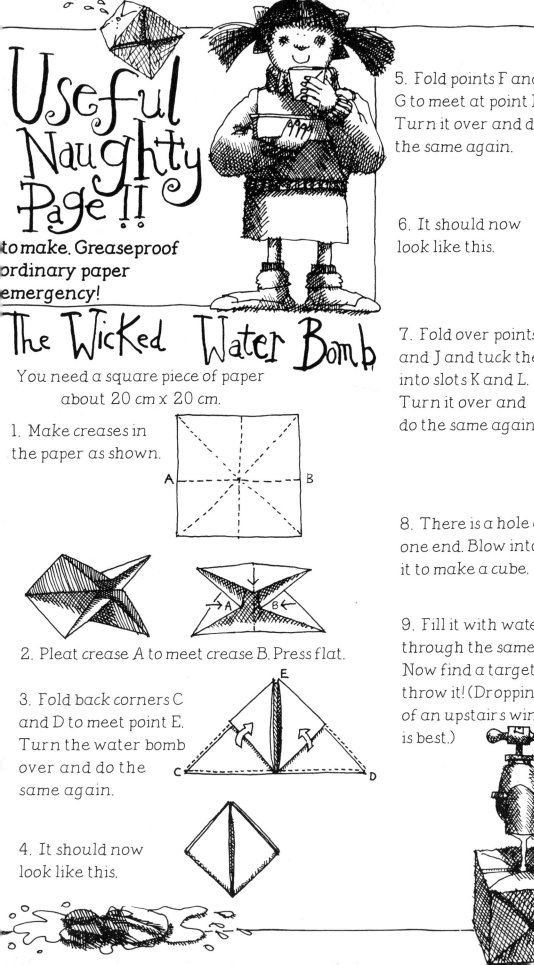

2. Pleat crease A to meet crease B. Press flat.

3. Fold back corners C
and D to meet point E.
Turn the water bomb
over and do the
same again.

4. It should now
look like this.

5. Fold points F and
G to meet at point H.
Turn it over and do
the same again.

6. It should now
look like this.

7. Fold over points I
and J and tuck them
into slots K and L.
Turn it over and
do the same again.

slot K

slot L

8. There is a hole at
one end. Blow into
it to make a cube.

9. Fill it with water
through the same cube.
Now find a target and
throw it! (Dropping it out
of an upstairs window
is best.)

hole

Finally, Pictures You Can Eat!

This is a yummy thing to do at a party or on your own.

You need a sheet of rice-paper attached to a piece of card with sticky tape, a teaspoon, pots containing different coloured icing and a selection of small, colourful sweets and edible cake decorations.

1. With the teaspoon, spread icing on the sheet of rice-paper.

2. Now press sweets and cake decorations into the icing.

3. Let the icing dry. Remove the card and sticky tape before eating your picture.

First published 1992 by
Walker Books Ltd
87 Vauxhall Walk
London SE11 5HJ
©1992 Alan Snow
The right of Alan Snow to be identified as author of this work
has been asserted by him in accordance with the Copyright,
Designs and Patents Act 1988.
Printed and bound in Great Britain
by Ebenezer Baylis Ltd, Worcester
British Library Cataloguing in Publication Data
A catalogue record for this book is
available from the British Library.
ISBN 0-7445-2236-6